Tiny Treasures

FICTION FROM
SOUTHERN SCOTLAND

First published in Great Britain in 2010 by
Young Writers, Remus House, Coltsfoot Drive,
Peterborough, PE2 9JX
Tel (01733) 890066 Fax (01733) 313524
Website: www.youngwriters.co.uk

Disclaimer
Young Writers has maintained every effort
to publish stories that will not cause offence.
Any stories, events or activities relating to individuals
should be read as fictional pieces and not construed
as real-life character portrayal.

Foreword

Since Young Writers was established in 1990, our aim has been to promote and encourage written creativity amongst children and young adults. By giving aspiring young authors the chance to be published, Young Writers effectively nurtures the creative talents of the next generation, allowing their confidence and writing ability to grow.

With our latest fun competition, *The Adventure Starts Here ...* , primary school children nationwide were given the tricky challenge of writing a story with a beginning, middle and an end in just fifty words.

The diverse and imaginative range of entries made the selection process a difficult but enjoyable task with stories chosen on the basis of style, expression, flair and technical skill. A fascinating glimpse into the imaginations of the future, we hope you will agree that this entertaining collection is one that will amuse and inspire the whole family.

Contents

**St Teresa's Primary School,
Newarthill**

The Mini Sagas

The Pirates Of The Caribbean

On June the 1st the Caribbean boat arrived.
People were pleased because it brought treasure.
Everyone was so excited. When the people came
out, Queen Elizabeth was very excited to see the
Caribbean boat. Queen Elizabeth was so pleased
she got on the boat and went to the lovely
Caribbean.

Lily Mitchell (8)
Aberdour Primary School, Aberdour

The Two Silly Pigs

One day there were two very silly pigs. They planned to blow up Fox who came a lot. They got a grenade, put it in a cannon.

One pig forgot and said, 'What's in here?' and suddenly *boom!* He went flying out. He died. 'Oops!' said the other pig.

Aidan Robertson (8)

Aberdour Primary School, Aberdour

The Big Bad Wolf Doesn't Like Pigs

One day the big bad wolf went on a lovely river walk. He saw three pigs drinking coffee. The three pigs were very gullible. So the big bad wolf said, 'Look, a magical dragon!' All the pigs looked around but the big bad wolf took the coffee and ran away.

David McDougall (9)
Aberdour Primary School, Aberdour

3

The Three Little Pigs

Three little pigs were building houses. The houses were made from bricks, bricks, cement, bricks, cement, steel. The wolf couldn't blow down the first two houses. He got a bomb, placed it in the third pig's house, *boom!* The wolf looked down and then said, 'How lovely, roasted pig, *yum!*'

Alistair Abbott (8)
Aberdour Primary School, Aberdour

Fat Riding Hood

One day it was Miss Riding Hood's birthday. She
was turning eight. She was expecting a cake. She
could not stop eating cake. Riding Hood's friends
were coming to see her for her party.
When they arrived the first thing they said was,
'Let's go and eat the cake now.'

Andreas Campbell (9)
Aberdour Primary School, Aberdour

Captain Skalywak's Ship

'Ahoy! Would you like to be the first to join my crew? Three meals a day, comfy cabins to sleep in,' lied Captain Skalywak. Over 60 people joined Captain Skalywak's voyage, but one person had to walk the plank every day. So Captain Skalywak's rotten boat set off to sea.

Ellen Baxter (9)
Aberdour Primary School, Aberdour

Our Chocolate World

Rebecca and Ellie woke up, everything was brown.

'We're in chocolate world,' said Rebecca. She tasted a leaf.

Ellie said, 'Yes.'

It was dark, Rebecca said, 'Can we go to sleep now?'

'OK.'

Next morning they were back in bed. Rebecca said, 'Did you dream about chocolate?

'Yes!' said Ellie.

Ellie-Rose Neilson (8)
Aberdour Primary School, Aberdour

7

Stranded

A long time ago, when the *Titanic* sank, lots of people drowned, but a very special child survived. She had managed to jump onto an iceberg to survive.

'Oh, I wish I had someone to talk to,' she said. Her name was Stephanie and she made friends with penguins.

Daisy Winskill (8)
Aberdour Primary School, Aberdour

My Cartoon Land

Jamie was playing in the garden.
'Ouch!' he said. He wasn't in his garden. Jamie
was scared. He saw the Simpsons. 'Where am I?'
Lisa replied, 'You are in Cartoon Land.'
'How do I get out of here?'
Marge said, 'You just go out here.'
Jamie was back. 'That was fun!'

Jamie Byrne (8)
Aberdour Primary School, Aberdour

9

The Disgusting Trick

Madeline was at school with her friends William
and Natalie. They were just walking until the bell
rang. William bent over. William grinned sneakily
while the girls chatted. The bell rang. *Squish!*
Madeline looked at her feet. William laughed. It
was his fake dog poo! It was William doing his
tricks.

Laura MacGregor (8)
Aberdour Primary School, Aberdour

The Two Little Dogs

Once there were two little dogs and a big cat that lived in a cartoon. The cat attacked the dogs with grenades, bombs and guns. Then when he was attacking the dogs he accidentally shot himself because he was facing the gun the wrong way, so now he is dead.

Adam Stevenson (8)
Aberdour Primary School, Aberdour

Everlasting Spring Chocolate

Once at the chocolate factory the owner, Natasha, was thinking of getting more workers to make more chocolate because everybody was buying it.

The next day people were barging into the factory to buy chocolate and asking to work there. She was pleased, so she opened a little shop.

Lucy Fraser (8)

Aberdour Primary School, Aberdour

At The Pub

On Sunday at 5.30pm my family called and I
had some dinner and a drink at the pub. Then I
watched the football till twenty-five minutes to
six. I had a vanilla ice cream, it was yummy.
On the way home I saw a huge UFO in the sky.

Blake Mewes (7)
Banton Primary School, Kilsyth

The Strange Creature

John was cold. The shipwreck that had just happened had been too much for him. He had crashed on some strange island in the middle of the Pacific Ocean. Suddenly, a huge fish with a horrific number of teeth jumped at him from the water. He dodged it. Close one!

Hamish Barrett (8)

Banton Primary School, Kilsyth

14

Lost

While I was on holiday in Blackpool with my family, I turned the corner of the toy shop and suddenly I lost sight of my mum and dad. I started to cry. The shopkeeper asked what happened, then, in the distance, I could see my parents. Thank goodness!

Caleb Watters (8)
Banton Primary School, Kilsyth

Fish, Dolphin And Mermaid

Katie, Emily and Kim dived into the water and
saw lots of colourful fish. They were clownfish,
crabs and dolphins. *It is brilliant,* thought Kim.
They saw a beautiful mermaid, it was amazing.
They said together when they came up to the top
of the water, 'Wow how amazing!'

Elena Walker (8)
Banton Primary School, Kilsyth

The Haunted House

Suddenly my ball rolled into the haunted house. Slowly I walked down the path. I opened the creaky door. A mouse ran in front of me! There I saw my ball. I ran along the wooden floor with the mouse behind me. I picked up my ball and ran. *Argh!*

Mhairi McFarlane (9)
Banton Primary School, Kilsyth

Hell

I was walking down a dark alley, I was alone. It was night, everything was still. Shadows were all around me, it was pitch-black. Shadows moved, I called, nobody answered. Someone grabbed me. I tried to scream but it was too late. I sank into a pool of darkness.

Kieran MacFarlane (9)
Banton Primary School, Kilsyth

The Haunted House

In King Street there is an ancient house, very ancient indeed. One day my friends and I got dared to go in. We went in, we shouted 'Argh! What is that?'
'It's a ghost,' I shouted, 'And there is a mummy! That's it, I am out of here!'

Hannah McFarlane (7)
Banton Primary School, Kilsyth

George The Giraffe

On my summer holidays I went to Edinburgh
Zoo with my family. It was a very sunny day. We
headed towards the giraffe enclosure to find
four long-necked giraffes. Suddenly I leaned over
to clap George the giraffe when he pinched my
baseball hat. I started screaming with shock!

William Ewan Chalmers (8)
Banton Primary School, Kilsyth

Haunted Castle

Sam drove to the dark mysterious castle. Inside he walked up the creaking stairs until he got to the master bedroom. *Thump!* What was that? Frightened Sam put the covers over his head. *Thump!* Was someone outside? Suddenly the door opened and a figure stood in the dark shadows …

William Ratchford (9)
Barrhill Primary School, Barrhill

Who's In The Darkness?

Where's my dad? He's two hours late. He should
have been back earlier. That looks like a car, it's
pulling over. That's not my dad, he's wearing a
white coat. Argh, there's blood dripping from his
hands. He's opening the door. *Noo!*
'Hi Son, sorry I'm late, hit a pheasant.'

Alexander Ratchford (11)
Barrhill Primary School, Barrhill

A Dark Gloomy Night

As I was walking through the dark woods, I heard twigs breaking beneath my feet. *Snap! Snap! Smash! What was that?* I thought. Before I had time to scream, a black figure approached me. I turned around. A flash of lightning filled the air. *Phew,* it was just a dream.

Courteney-Jayne Flower (11)
Barrhill Primary School, Barrhill

The Castle

One dark night a boy was playing with his friend,
they ended up at an old ruined castle and found
a football to play with. At the back of the castle
they played footy. Suddenly they heard the
rattling of chains, the door swung open - a huge
man stood there …

Johnathan Gray (11)
Barrhill Primary School, Barrhill

The Bright White Figure

One day I walked past an old wicked castle and saw a white figure glaring at me. I thought it was my imagination at first, so I went for a closer look. I was absolutely terrified. My hand trembled. What was it? Oh! It was a boy from my class!

Katherine McCarthy (9)
Barrhill Primary School, Barrhill

Untitled

I was coming back from my friend's house to go
back home when I saw a big black shadow at the
door. I screamed! I yelled! I ran away home! I
jumped into bed! I was back home safe.
When I woke up it was all a dream. Oh *phew!*

Emily Miles (10)
Barrhill Primary School, Barrhill

The Strange Noise

One night Samantha was camping. She heard a strange noise. She unzipped her tent and went out with her torch. She saw a shadow in the trees. She shone her torch in the trees. It was a rubbish bag moving in the wind. She smiled and went back to sleep.

Bethany Flanagan (11)
Blairdardie Primary School, Glasgow

When Humpty Got Owned

Humpty-Dumpty sat on a wall. Humpty-Dumpty fell off his wall and fell and fell and fell and *splat!* All the king's horses and all the king's men had eggs for breakfast, lunch and dinner until the year 2010. Unlucky Humpty-Dumpty, you got owned.

Callum McCammon (11)
Blairdardie Primary School, Glasgow

The 31st Of October

One day on the 31st of October I walked outside.
It was dark and clammy. People in costumes
swarmed the streets.
Later that night there was a howl. I froze in fear
and ran home. I tripped and stumbled. I had to
tell Mum and Dad - nothing else mattered.

Jamie Forrester (11)
Blairdardie Primary School, Glasgow

King Arthur Marries A Princess

King Arthur was a famous king. He was great at
fighting and good at using weapons.
One day he was going to marry a princess in a big
castle. He couldn't wait to marry her. They had a
great wedding day and lived happily ever after.

Scott Haynes (11)
Blairdardie Primary School, Glasgow

Thumbelina And The Bee

There was a fairy called Thumbelina. One sunny
day she was looking out the window when she
heard a bee. The bee flew into the house and
took her to the hive. Thumbelina fell out of the
hive. The bee chased her and she flapped her way
back home.

Amy Burrows (11)
Blairdardie Primary School, Glasgow

Hell Is Unleashed

Jimmy was finally home. As he entered his house, he realised that it was covered in webs and it was cold. There were chessboards everywhere in every room. As he walked up to his parents he noticed it was hot. He turned the doorknob and Hell was unleashed!

Darren McLaughlin (11)
Blairdardie Primary School, Glasgow

Bieber Fever

There was a girl walking down Bieber Street. There were fans outside his house. They were screaming and shouting and they were shouting, 'Justin Bieber' and 'We want Justin Bieber.' There were posters and banners everywhere. It was a blast. They were there all day and all night.

Megan McKay (11)
Blairdardie Primary School, Glasgow

Return Of Hellhound

It was a dark day. Suddenly I saw a flash of light going across the sky. Then the skies opened up and a fireball landed on top of me. I was going to die. I did die and the end of the world was very close.

Joshua Kenny (11)
Blairdardie Primary School, Glasgow

34

A Twist In A Tale

One day a boy made a twist in a tale. He said Humpty-Dumpty sat on a swing, swung all day, then he fell off and broke his nail. He was in a bad way. A boy saw it and called 999. Humpty-Dumpty was fine without a nail.

Thomas Whelan (11)

Blairdardie Primary School, Glasgow

Once Upon A Night

Once upon a night a boy dreamt about a dinosaur.
It tried to bite him but he punched the dinosaur.
That didn't work so he stabbed it, but again it
didn't work so he got a chainsaw and cut its head
open. Then he got a gun and shot it.

Sam Carlin (11)

Blairdardie Primary School, Glasgow

In The Park

I was running through the park when I saw something race by me then it disappeared. I was panicking so I kept running until I got home. I told my mum about it but she said the same old boring stuff, 'There are no such things as ghosts.'

David Graham (11)
Blairdardie Primary School, Glasgow

The Adventures Of A Hobo

There was a hobo called Leon. He was very poor and hungry. One day he was leaning over the canal and fell in. Then he got a plastic bag stuck on his head and died. RIP Leon the hobo.

Elisha McClymont (11)

Blairdardie Primary School, Glasgow

The Dog, The Cat And The Egg

Yesterday it was my birthday and I got tickets to
see a dog, cat and an egg singing and dancing.
'Oh my God!' I said because the concert was sold
out.
The next day I went to the concert, it was great. I
thought the egg was the best.

Steven Merry (11)
Blairdardie Primary School, Glasgow

39

Adventures Of The Cat And The Zombie

I was watching a film about zombies one night
when I heard a chap at the window. I was that
scared I went and got my dad. I told him, 'I think
there is a zombie at the window.' My dad opened
the window and in came my cat.

Kurt De Smet (11)
Blairdardie Primary School, Glasgow

The Day I Got Hit By A Car And Died

One day I was walking down the road. The next minute I smelled ice cream and walked across the road. Unfortunately I hadn't seen the wet cement sign. Then I got hit by a car and died.
The next day I came back as a zombie and killed the town.

Cameron Mitchell (11)
Blairdardie Primary School, Glasgow

Incy Wincy Spider Volume 2

Incy Wincy Spider climbed up the rusty spout.
He was halfway there and the water came down.
Incy hung on by a leg, the leg came off and Incy
fell down. He landed in a dog's mouth and that
was the end of Incy Wincy Spider and the dog
too!

Arron Scott (11)

Blairdardie Primary School, Glasgow

42

Midnight Mansion

In 1877, a girl went into a supposedly haunted
mansion at midnight, but she never came out.
100 years later, two girls went into the now
crumbling mansion to find a skeleton and a
Victorian dress. Suddenly there was a loud
bang and then there were two new skeletons,
haunting.

Rebecca Pellow (11)
Blairdardie Primary School, Glasgow

43

Careless

I was crossing the road and an animal caught my eye. I walked towards it; I was so busy trying to get over the road that I lost where the animal went! Not looking where I was going I fell down a hole and broke both my legs and arms.

Alanna Kirk (11)
Blairdardie Primary School, Glasgow

Unit

I was at war in 1942. One day an enemy soldier
captured me and took me as a prisoner of war.
A week later I was executed by Corporal Dunn.
The next week Captain MacTavish came to the
rescue but was too late; my crippled remains
were on the ground.

Sam Riddell (11)

Blairdardie Primary School, Glasgow

A Story About Elisha

Once upon a time there was a girl called Elisha
who lived in a box near the canal. At night she
slept in the box but accidentally she rolled into
the canal and happily she died and she was never
found.

Carla Hossack (11)
Blairdardie Primary School, Glasgow

The Wolf

As Victoria walked into the abandoned office she heard spooky whispers. It was Halloween and she was all alone. She crept upstairs and hovered in the doorway before she was disturbed by creaky floorboards. Suddenly a wild wolf jumped out behind her and chased her to her deadly doom.

Chloe Hendry (12)
Blairdardie Primary School, Glasgow

My Blood

Tremors ran through my body as I felt his cool
breath on my neck. I turned round to see his
bloodthirsty red eyes, and his sharp fangs. His
arms were entangled around me - I couldn't
move. Just then, his marble skin reached my neck.
Then, the vampire bit me.

Brooke Shields (11)
Blairdardie Primary School, Glasgow

48

Startled

My heart pounded as cold hands trapped me in
their grasp. I turned around to see a motionless
face staring back. His eyes were an unfamiliar
colour. I was startled, too startled to say anything.
He let me free from his grasp and I finally took in
the beautiful figure.

Hannah Clark Foster (11)
Blairdardie Primary School, Glasgow

Nazi Zombies

I was in my room with my friends playing my
scary Nazi zombie game. One of the zombies
sneaked up behind my character (Tank) and
attacked him! I jumped and screamed and my
friends laughed at me. The power cut, the lights
flickered and my friends vanished.
'Who's laughing now?'

Jack Blair (11)
Blairdardie Primary School, Glasgow

Day In The Life Of Arnie

One day me and Josh went to see Arnie about the
film. We got to see the film, it was cool!
After that we got dinner and went on the Xbox
then went to bed.

Cameron Milligan (11)
Blairdardie Primary School, Glasgow

Return Of Jason X

It was Saturday night in Reigen Street. It was loud, dark and there was a killer on the loose. We called him Jason X. He died when he was 13 and he killed anyone who got in his way. Finally, he met his end when he was drowned.

William Gibson (11)

Blairdardie Primary School, Glasgow

The Tennis Surprise

The thunder was terrifying, the wind was battering Mike. A mysterious figure had been following him all day. It pulled out a bat and tried to get Mike. Mike ran to his house. The door was locked. He tried the back door.
'Are you coming to table tennis?' said Ashley.

Tadiwanashe Muzambi (9)
Craigroyston Primary School, Edinburgh

Vampire Blood

One stormy night Nicole was in the woods when she heard a scream. The wind grew colder. A bat flew out and turned into a vampire. It grabbed Nicole and sucked every drop of blood from her body.
I'm not reading this book any more; it's too scary for me.

Melissa Hughes (10)
Craigroyston Primary School, Edinburgh

Stuck In Space

They were stuck in the middle of deep space. No one could help them now they thought and they were right. There was something on the roof. The roof fell in. It crushed the astronauts. Luckily it was a dream, but the next day, *thud, thud, thud* on the roof!

Amber Hagley (9)
Craigroyston Primary School, Edinburgh

55

In The Dark Scary Forest

I suddenly realised I was lost. I was worried.
There were trees surrounding me everywhere. I
couldn't tell which way to go; all the paths looked
the same. I was really frightened. Someone
touched me on the arm.
'Hello little girl in the red cloak,' said a huge hairy
wolf.

Courtney Wilson (10)
Craigroyston Primary School, Edinburgh

Untitled

Darcey was in the woods. Going home she thought something was watching her. She could hear footsteps so she ran. Someone was there. She sprinted to a hole in a tree to hide. Suddenly a voice, 'Darcey, I've been looking for you. Where've you been?' said her friend Amy.

Tiegan McGraw (10)
Craigroyston Primary School, Edinburgh

57

The Jungle

I suddenly realised I was lost in here. In the jungle, giant leaves were in my face. I stepped in gooey stuff. I heard strange noises so I grabbed a vine and swung like a monkey and landed. I ran. I saw the glow of a village. I was safe.

Caitlin McArdle (10)

Craigroyston Primary School, Edinburgh

The Leprechaun

Two people were walking down a road.
Suddenly a leprechaun jumped out, he was called
Hornswoggle. Shawn and Hunter were terrified,
then the leprechaun said, 'Daa.'
Hunter said, *'Phew!'*
Then they went to wrestling and won a match.
Then they made DX. They won every match
after and parted.

Connor Reid (10)
Craigroyston Primary School, Edinburgh

My Little Fairy

I'm sure I saw a fairy; she was floating around my
room.
Mum said, 'It's just your imagination.'
Dad said, 'Be quiet, I'm watching TV.'
My little sister said, 'Cool, wow, tell me what she
looked like.'
'She's beautiful, tiny and colourful,' I explained.
'Come meet her, you'll love her.'

Naomi Fleming (10)
Garelochhead Primary School, Garelochhead

School Day

Tuesday at school, all of the class ran to the
window and found Cinderella sitting on a wall.
She fell off the wall and broke her heel; we
all found it really funny. After that we all got
working.
After, we played a game then stopped. Then all
went home.

Cara McQueen (10)
Garelochhead Primary School, Garelochhead

The Haunted House

One dark night, me and my friend, Charlie, went
to a haunted house. At the house, we saw ghosts,
vampires and bats. It was really scary but that was
only downstairs, then we went upstairs. When
we were upstairs, it was really freaky. Then we
decided to go home.

Andrew Aitken (9)
Garelochhead Primary School, Garelochhead

Wobbly Jelly!

Wobbly jelly was in my bowl, covered with ice cream. I looked at it deciding on how to eat it. Should I put my spoon in the middle or should I eat a little bit from the side? I sat there looking at my wobbly jelly. Should I eat it?

Amy Dobrijevic (10)
Garelochhead Primary School, Garelochhead

The Killer Toon

It was a horrific day for Eddie and his brother
Tim. A piano was rushing straight towards them.
Eddie couldn't make out the whole toon but he
could see that it had red eyes. Suddenly the piano
hit them. Tim died, Eddie broke his arm.

Bobby James Brabender (10)
Garelochhead Primary School, Garelochhead

The Fairy Tale Remix!

Cinderella went to a ball and sat on a wall; off she fell and broke her arm. The prince fell about laughing. The ambulance was there in a flash. Cinderella took out her phone and called her mum, started crying, realising her mum was in Spain.

Melanie Tipping (11)

Garelochhead Primary School, Garelochhead

Sonic

There was once a dog called Sonic. He was living in a house in Town Square. Sonic was kicked out of his house because he was vicious. A boy and girl found Sonic and took him home.

Liam Rogers (9)

Garelochhead Primary School, Garelochhead

What Is Life?

'What is life?' asked Alex.
'Go away!' Kate shouted.
'Fine!' Alex said fiercely. He went to his little
room to think. *Life, funny thing,* he thought. Then
Alex sprung up. 'Life is about going your way.' he
said aloud. 'Now I can live life smoothly.'

Isabelle Innocent (9)
Garelochhead Primary School, Garelochhead

Bird's Nest

Once there was a girl who went for a walk in a forest. On her walk she climbed a tree. On the tree there was a bird's nest. In the bird's nest there were baby chicks. One baby chick fell out so the girl took it home to mend it.

Tieghan Pryde (9)
Gateside Primary School, Gateside

Mountain Rescue

I was at the top of the mountain. My hair was blowing everywhere, my eyes were watering. I was very tired. I heard a bark, it sounded like a dog. I followed the bark, it led to a cave. Inside the cave there was a dog. I took it home.

Sarani Fernando (9)

Gateside Primary School, Gateside

69

Self Service

About two years ago I was walking to the shop
when I realised it'd moved to the other side of
the street. I went over to it. *Right, what's on my
list? Milk and bread.* Found the bread, asked for
milk, saw a cow - self service! It's the Milky Way.

Matthew Allan (10)
Gateside Primary School, Gateside

Gone

Happy, that's how I was feeling when I came home from the party. Well, I was until I noticed that my parents had vanished. They were gone! I checked all the rooms but they weren't there. Then the phone rang. It was my mum and dad saying, 'You alright?'

Robbie Struth (11)

Gateside Primary School, Gateside

The Mission

Five, four, three, two, one, blast off! We zoomed
past Venus and landed on Mercury where we
found aliens of all shapes and sizes. Some were
big and some were tall but they were mostly
small. None could speak proper English so we
had to turn back. The mission failed!

Evelyn Morgan (10)
Gateside Primary School, Gateside

Halloween

One spooky Halloween I wasn't allowed out
and my mum went out. I heard a knock at the
door, I opened it. It was the headless horseman!
He chased me all over my house and I hid in the
cupboard. When I came out he had magically
disappeared.

Anelie Ramage (8)
Glengowan Primary School, Caldercruix

Zoo

One day I went to the zoo. When I got there
I saw lots of monkeys, tigers and lions. Then a
peacock started to chase me. I was scared and I
ran away. Finally I ran back to my mum and dad
and we came home.

Amy McKee (8)
Glengowan Primary School, Caldercruix

Sanctuary

Once, in a land called Northburn, there was a sanctuary where magical creatures lived in harmony. The dark overlord invaded Northburn, broke into the sanctuary and smashed it up and found new minions. There were five minions to help the overlord to become lord of the world.

Arran Adams (9)
Glengowan Primary School, Caldercruix

The Lost Kitten

Once, there was a kitten called Oliver. His coat
was black and his eyes were a glamorous green.
One day Oliver didn't come home. I went out to
find him and Oliver surprised me by jumping out
of a tree!

Olivia Ferguson (9)
Glengowan Primary School, Caldercruix

An Adventure Home

One day a boy called Calum was walking home
from school when he met Francis, the school
bully. So Calum ran until he got home and
scampered up to his room and pinched himself.
'Ooh! It was all just a dream. I better get some
sleep for school tomorrow.'

Calum Keelan (9)
Kelty Primary School, Kelty

The Surprise

On 20th July 2007 on my birthday, Mia, Fay and
my family came with me for a surprise to Blair
Drummond Safari Park to see all of the animals
and go on the rides. It was a very, very, very good
day at the mystery surprise.

Joshua Sneddon (9)

Kelty Primary School, Kelty

Granny's House

Sasha was extremely nervous about staying at her granny's house. At night she kept on hearing weeping sounds. Sasha was too terrified to even move a muscle. She tried to scream but she couldn't. She bolted out of her bed and ran down the stairs to the basement for safety.

Emma Young (10)
King's Road Primary School, Dunfermline

Norma's Death

Norma slowly walked back into the old shed
looking very confused. The spiders had multiplied;
there were at least a dozen of them. She had no
idea what to do. Norma slashed her way through
the spiders. Blood was dripping everywhere. The
spiders weren't dying, the girl was. Silence.

Ciara Ireland (10)
King's Road Primary School, Dunfermline

Ghost In The Cupboard

Annie lay in her bed staring at the horrifying pair of eyes that glared at her. Suddenly it flew straight through the cupboard door. The ghost hovered above Annie's head and its whisper echoed in her ear. The ghost's long raggedy hair brushed against Annie's face. *Swish!* It slowly disappeared.

Caitlin Day (10)
King's Road Primary School, Dunfermline

The Stolen Crown

The thief had found it, the location of the queen's crown. Chuckling, she slithered across the roof using her quiet, no-mess cutter to slice the tiles and insulation. Then, attaching her harness to the roof, she slid down. Without warning she detached her harness and, grabbing the crown, ran.

Breege Fraser (11)
King's Road Primary School, Dunfermline

The President's Disappearance

Owen had his disguise on, feeling dark and
evil inside. 'Perfect!' he exclaimed with
unpleasantness. It was time to take control of the
President of the United States.
At the White House the building was heavily
guarded. Owen got in and found him. Nobody
ever saw the President again.

Kyle Walker (10)
King's Road Primary School, Dunfermline

The Evil Creatures

The bright light flickered. Darkness. Silence. Ciara
was scared as she walked to the deadly forest.
She was halfway through when she saw a cottage.
After a second, Ciara crept past and the door
squeaked. Something breathed behind Ciara.
Ciara was cold and fainted on the mouldy ground.

Kiana Reid (10)

King's Road Primary School, Dunfermline

84

A Spider's Wrath

Tanith jumped off the wall, her sword glowing with the fluorescent spider's blood. Her sword lashed out and sliced the emperor spider's arm off. Its giant claw struck her chest, sending her to the ground. Death was sneaking up on her and fast. Her grip loosened and her sword fell.

Liam Burke (10)

King's Road Primary School, Dunfermline

Moor Of Death

Bowen stood still on the moor as two red eyes
watched him. The stench of rotting flesh was
getting closer. Then he saw a dark green creature,
a fat ogre. It was covered in the bones of other
mythical creatures. The ogre looked at Bowen,
raised his fist and roared.

Maciej Denicki (10)
King's Road Primary School, Dunfermline

My Evil Brother

I was in my house watching TV while my little
brother was poking my arm.
'Leave me alone! He does that all the time,' I
mumbled, I went up to my room and I was pacing
up and down. What should my revenge be? *Ah ha!
I'll scare him. Ha!*

Amber Donaldson (10)
King's Road Primary School, Dunfermline

The Dark Woods

Aah! He twisted his foot badly as he limped out of the hole. There were more of them so he tried to run fast. Loads of them came as he rolled down the hill. It was getting dark. He felt really scared. He had to go back.

Cameron Black (11)
King's Road Primary School, Dunfermline

The Killer Ghost

The footsteps were getting louder. As a pair of
red eyes appeared something was touching Scott
on the shoulder. He shrieked as he felt it. A yell
from behind made him want to run. Scott's bones
cracked and he collapsed. There was a scream
and a sudden death for him.

Louise Durham (10)

King's Road Primary School, Dunfermline

She-Devil

I shook my head. Was I dreaming? I heard the
voice of the she-devil. Oh no, I couldn't move,
what was I going to do? I needed to try to get up
or I'd be down in the rumbling stomach of the
she-devil. *Argh!*

Sian Lewis (11)
King's Road Primary School, Dunfermline

The Haunted House

Mark approached the eerie house. He climbed the unstable steps towards the door.
'Hello?' said the boy.
'Who's there?' said a voice. The door opened and Mark very regretfully went inside. Without warning, something came out of nowhere and grabbed him and took him away. Nobody ever saw him again.

Sean Heron (10)
King's Road Primary School, Dunfermline

The Spider's Death

Jake shivered as the slimy green goo ran off his sword. Something scuttled across the floor. Jake dashed out of the room leaving the spiders lurking in the shadows. Suddenly one of them pounced on Jake. He pulled out his sword and stabbed it. Jake watched as it lay lifeless.

Cara Wilson (10)

King's Road Primary School, Dunfermline

The Lost Gold

On holiday Sean found a box of gold. He picked it up and suddenly *bang!* Sean dropped it again. He didn't know what to do. He thought to himself, *should I take it?* Suddenly it was not there. The gold was gone. Sean was shocked. Where did it go?

Kenneth Anderson (10)
King's Road Primary School, Dunfermline

The Spider's Death

John instantly drew the sword from its sheath and
slashed at the spiders. Two of them were killed
before the last one fled. The blood was coming
down the spider's neck. John put his sword
down.

Coral Henry (10)
King's Road Primary School, Dunfermline

94

Bill's Disappearance

The ghost played with Bill like he was a toy. It was too swift to see with the naked eye. Bill could hear it chuckle at him.

'Oh no!' Bill screamed. 'I've been covered in slime by the ghost.' The slime made Bill disappear. Nobody saw Bill after that day.

Mark Smith (10)

King's Road Primary School, Dunfermline

Tank Attack!

The tank rumbled through the darkness. It fired
and splinters went flying. Richard ran to the
nearest foxhole. His friend, Private McClusky, let
out a scream of pain. McClusky had been killed by
a splinter in his neck. American tanks came from
behind and finished the German tank.

Andrew McRae Wheeler (10)
King's Road Primary School, Dunfermline

The Shadow

A sunny day loomed over Paris as Colleen was
trapped in an abandoned building. Suddenly an
arm reached out and grabbed her. A shadow
emerged from the darkness.
'I'm here to save you,' said the shadow in a low
profile. They fled out of the building and over the
horizon.

Aysling MacKenzie (10)
King's Road Primary School, Dunfermline

Blood In The Dragon's Den

Andrew lunged at the dragon, blood dripping
from the edge of his blade. Crimson flames
roared from the dragon's mouth, scorching
Andrew's hand. He screamed with anger, his
sword lashing out for the final blow. Andrew
stabbed the dragon's stomach; shrieks pierced the
air like blades. The dragon fell. Dead.

Morgan Braid (10)
King's Road Primary School, Dunfermline

The Haunted House

When Daniel was at the front door there was
a note that said, 'Come in!' Suddenly the door
automatically opened. When he walked in, the
door slammed shut. He was scared stiff. Daniel
tried to open the door, but it was locked.
'Help! Help! Help!' Daniel screamed.

Euan Turner (10)
King's Road Primary School, Dunfermline

Grandma Brown

It grew colder and colder in the dark night.
'Grandma, where are you?' There was no reply.
Suddenly an old crooked voice said, 'I'm over
here Leah.' Leah went closer and closer to the
voice. She struggled her way over the moors to
her grandma and struggled home.

Rebecca Birt (10)
King's Road Primary School, Dunfermline

The Escape

Luke slid down to the cellar of the school, he'd never known about it. Apparently there was an exit out of the school. He glanced around the room - old homework files and the exit. He crawled through the narrow passage out to the playground to find … the head teacher.

Amy-Louise Rogers (10)
King's Road Primary School, Dunfermline

Lola Rabbit Saves The Day

One day, Lola Rabbit was playing in the garden when she heard squealing. Molly Mouse was stuck in a mousetrap. Lola unclipped it and Molly gave a sigh of relief as her tail wriggled with freedom. Molly and Lola went home and were careful not to get caught again.

Ellysse Swainson (11)

King's Road Primary School, Dunfermline

Haunted House

At the haunted house, Bob was walking through
the garden. It had tombstones. Bob walked into
the house. He heard a voice in the background.
'RIP' it said.
Bob was scared, he tried to escape but the doors
slammed shut. He shouted 'Help!' No one heard
him … he didn't survive.

Jamie McArthur (11)
King's Road Primary School, Dunfermline

Brian's First Adventure

He walked and walked for hours then suddenly
Brian noticed something, a big black hole in the
cliff. It was a cave but it had huge pawprints
leading inside.
'I always wanted an adventure,' Brian said. 'So
now I have one!' He stumbled inside and … was a
bear's lunch!

Chloe Knight (11)
King's Road Primary School, Dunfermline

Evacuation

The train was full of children; I looked around and
saw my teacher Mrs Govener put a large bit of
paper on my jacket. Then she pushed me onto a
seat and said, 'Sit down there.'
When we reached our destination I didn't like it, I
wanted to go home.

Keli Dalrymple (11)
King's Road Primary School, Dunfermline

Invasion Of The Nazis

Boom! The Nazis dropped bombs. All you could
hear were the air raid sirens. People were
screaming while running. Planes were flying
through the sky. People in the shelters were so
frightened they had to sit next to each other.
Smashed up houses at the end of the first war.

Conor Jones (11)
King's Road Primary School, Dunfermline

A Mirror In The Funhouse

At the fair Olivia's favourite place was always
deserted, the Fun House. Olivia adored the room
of mirrors. She thought today would be normal,
but as she entered the mirror room, a hand
covered her mouth.
Nowadays if you look into the clown mirror,
Olivia is in there staring back.

Chelsea Russell (11)
King's Road Primary School, Dunfermline

Random

It was the first time I had ever seen a jelly baby, then it came alive and said, 'Hi guys, how you doing?'
'OK.' It was weird. It then fried a Haribo egg and ate it! I have never seen such a random thing.

Lewis McDonald (11)
King's Road Primary School, Dunfermline

108

Home Time

It's the last day of school. It is only 10 minutes
until home time. Suddenly the fire alarm goes off.
We go out of school for 5 minutes. Finally the
alarm goes off. We go inside.
It is only 1 minute till home time then … *ring* …
ring. Freedom!

Laura Peden (11)
King's Road Primary School, Dunfermline

Stick Boy

Once this little boy called Thomas, only three,
had lots of crayons. Up in his messy bedroom,
after dinner, he was looking around his room for
his violet crayon. He liked drawing, especially on
walls. He found it.
The next day there were drawings on the walls.
He was gone.

Danielle Todd (11)

King's Road Primary School, Dunfermline

What A Cheapskate - Tooth Fairy And Santa

The tooth fairy crept in, put a penny under my pillow. I woke up, checked, two pence. What a cheapskate!
It was Christmas, I went downstairs to see my presents - only one! What a cheapskate.
Easter time! I went downstairs to see my eggs - only one, cheapskate!

Michael Hadley (11)
King's Road Primary School, Dunfermline

The Dragon Slayer

David approached the cave to kill his worst
enemy, the dragon. He entered the cave on his
horse, Teemo. The dragon was fast. Suddenly the
dragon awoke. Its fire roared from its mouth.
David drew his sword and sliced the dragon. The
dragon fled from the cave. David was furious.

Aaron Inkster (10)

King's Road Primary School, Dunfermline

Plain Sailing

It was two o'clock when we went sailing in Mistral. We ported off at the ferry and were four miles away from Inchkeith Island. We were almost at Incholm, water was over the gunnels with the force five winds. Papa Phil was amazed. Surprise! The boom swept me overboard. *Damn!*

Mackie Hughes (11)
King's Road Primary School, Dunfermline

Dragon's Cove

I approached the horrific beast; it was black and
ten metres long. I was steps away when it moved.
Its eyes opened and it roared. It spewed out blue
fire. It burnt my arm, but that didn't stop me, I
drew my sword and faced the beast. Everything
went black.

Owen Agnew (11)
King's Road Primary School, Dunfermline

114

The Mysterious Noises

Johnny was in bed. The front door opened and slammed shut! The floorboards started squeaking and there was the sound of smashing glass. The stairs started squeaking and there was a thud on Johnny's door. Johnny ran out to see Dad.
'You scared me!' Johnny said.
'Sorry,' said Dad.

Conner Harvey (11)
King's Road Primary School, Dunfermline

115

Christmas Morning

I tiptoed cautiously down the stairs and, as
always, stepped over the creaky stair. I slowly
opened the lounge door trying not to make a
sound. I took a big step into the lounge. As the
Christmas lights twinkled they reflected off of all
the shiny boxes of presents. *Wow!*

Sophy Dowie (11)
King's Road Primary School, Dunfermline

The Cliff

I was standing on a cliff when I felt something push me. The next thing I knew, I was falling, falling like I was never going to stop. 'Argh!' I screamed. Suddenly I opened my eyes, I was back in my room. It was all a dream.

Sophie Duguid (11)
King's Road Primary School, Dunfermline

My Love Story

Oh my! I woke up this morning feeling distracted.
'Wow, look at that chair, fresh,' I whispered under
my breath. Oh my God. I couldn't believe it - I
felt like I was in love, but not with a chair, a nicely
dressed pink box! I kissed it, *ooh, she's nice!*

Reece Dobbin (11)
King's Road Primary School, Dunfermline

The Pixies' Forest

I began my walk through the forest and listened to the sound of the birds tweeting. I sat down to eat my picnic when I saw a beautiful creature fly past my foot. It was a pixie! Several more came and began to dance; I couldn't help but join in ...

Jemma Dawson (11)
King's Road Primary School, Dunfermline

The Biggest Task

There I was, shunted with the most impossible task ever! It was worse than fighting lions or dragons or even the Loch Ness monster! All alone in the house, I trudged up the stairs to my brother's room. I had to clean his shoes!

Mehak Choudhary (11)
King's Road Primary School, Dunfermline

120

The Thesaurus

I was sitting at my desk, figuring out how to spell
a particularly hard word, when a huge dinosaur
came crashing through the side of the school,
came up to me and said, 'Hello, I'm a thesaurus,
what are you stuck on?'
'This word,' I replied and pointed to it.

Keira Lightning (11)
King's Road Primary School, Dunfermline

My Creepy Holiday

I reached my holiday cottage. I stepped inside, it ponged. There were cobwebs everywhere and then a shock came to my eyes - there was a nest of black falcons. They looked at me disgustedly. I looked back ... they attacked. I struggled, got them off me and ran for my life.

Robert Brookes (11)
King's Road Primary School, Dunfermline

Me And Robert Had Lunch
At Greggs The Bakers

Me and Robert were walking to Greggs when
suddenly a car smashed into Marinis. We laughed
because it was a red Ford Focus. Then we went
into Greggs and bought lunch, then we saw the
police coming. We stood there watching, also
eating our big lunch and drinking Lucozade. *Yum!*

Scott Wilson (11)

King's Road Primary School, Dunfermline

My Great Birthday

Today it is my birthday, I am 11 years old. I got 9 cards and a new phone, some clothes and some make-up. I had a chocolate cake. Then I had a white chocolate at my nana's. I got a cross stitching kit too. It was great fun.

Brooke Stewart (11)
King's Road Primary School, Dunfermline

Bombing Raid

Three, two, one - *vroom* goes one of the planes.
Suddenly another plane goes, but before the third
one can go, *bang, bang, boom* go the bombs of
German bombers. This is not a test drive.
'2 on 7,' says one of the drivers. Suddenly, get to
corner - a nuke!

Myles Fyvie (10)
King's Road Primary School, Dunfermline

Untitled

'Fe, fi, fo, fum, I smell a little one.' Jack ran as fast as he could. He was climbing down the beanstalk. He heard a chopping noise then the beanstalk fell.

Laura Cheney-Mack (10)
King's Road Primary School, Dunfermline

Metalboy And Acidgirl

Two kids got mutated during their sleep, one boy and one girl. The next day they were called Metalboy and Acidgirl. They were heroes. They beat every villain that stood in their way, except the Bonecrusher. Nothing could stop him. It was their biggest test. Already London was destroyed.

Kyle Burt (10)
King's Road Primary School, Dunfermline

Untitled

'Attack! Argh!' *Bang, bang, bang!* Jets everywhere.
The British had over 100,000 men but we've lost
5,000 men in a blink of an eye. We have to take
over Germany. Germany only have 76,000 men,
but we'll still try our best to defeat them.
Finally they are defeated, finally.

David Cunningham (10)
King's Road Primary School, Dunfermline

The Big Green Stalk

'Fe, fi, fo, fum,' I heard a noise in the garden. It was a green stalk. 'Come down and talk to me!' I said. My dad came out and cut the stalk down. He fell down. 'No dad!' It was a giant.

Amy Pearson (10)
King's Road Primary School, Dunfermline

The Bad Dream

The street was dark. Suddenly the lights went on.
All Mark could see were zombies. He ran for his
life. The zombies were in front of him. He had no
escape. All the zombies jumped onto Mark.
He woke up - it was all a bad dream.

Harris Buchanan (10)
King's Road Primary School, Dunfermline

Jumping John

In the year 3000 a boy called John could jump high.
One day John wanted a challenge so he went to the top of a building and wanted to jump across to the other. The distance was about 50 metres. He jumped and that was the end of jumping John.

Jamie Wilson (10)
King's Road Primary School, Dunfermline

The Evil Dragons

Crash! The whole house felt like it was moving.
Tom was hiding under the bed.
'Tom, get out from under the bed,' said Mum.
Tom went downstairs to see what the noise was.
Suddenly Tom saw three dragons standing in front
of him. They were going to eat him!

Natasha Webb (10)
King's Road Primary School, Dunfermline

132

A Twisted Tale

'Fe, fi, fi, fum' roared the giant. Jack dived down the beanstalk. The giant climbed down after him. When Jack got to the bottom he saw the giant. When the giant got down he stood on a magical flower patch and turned into a fairy. Jack made fun of him!

Alicia Ready (10)
King's Road Primary School, Dunfermline

The Legend Of Flyboy

In 1486 there was a superhero known as Flyboy.
He saved mankind and children in need from
evil doers, until a new enemy called Bloodspike
appeared. The two fighters were fighting for 524
years until it came to a conclusion. For the first
time ever, Flyboy was defeated!

Hugh Moorhead (10)
King's Road Primary School, Dunfermline

134

The Fatal Shot

Three, two, one and *splash,* the ramp crashed down on the beach. Jackson was 19 and he was forced to join the army. He was a sniper on D-Day and his life was about to end. He was about to take a shot when a landmine ended his life.

Ewan Morgan (10)
King's Road Primary School, Dunfermline

Frightened

There was a creak in the floor but no one was there. I ran straight to my mum and dad's room but they were dead! So I ran to the kitchen, I found a big knife. Then I set up traps but then I heard another creak …

Kayleigh Potter (10)
King's Road Primary School, Dunfermline

Untitled

'Fe, fi, fo, fum!'
'The giant is coming, help me!' shouted Jackie.
Jackie ran down the beanstalk and ran into the
house screaming! The giant was halfway down the
beanstalk and down the giant fell, down, down,
down.

Jemma Wilson (10)
King's Road Primary School, Dunfermline

Untitled

'Who is in my house?'
'Run!' shouted the giant's wife.
'Who is in my house?'
'Run, Jack, run!'
'OK.' Jack slid down the beanstalk, 'Get an axe
Mum!' Jack jumped off the beanstalk and his mum
chopped it down.

Jack Edwards (10)
King's Road Primary School, Dunfermline

Big Bill

One cold icy day, the school bully, Big Bill, was
coming towards me looking angry.
'What are you staring at?'
'Me, I, nothing Bill.' Bill cracked his knuckles,
drew nearer and I leaned well back. He looked
down on me with anger in his eyes.
'You're going down little man!'

Jake Gray (11)
King's Road Primary School, Dunfermline

Dead Man Walking

As the midnight hour approached, Albert Einstein
rose from his grave for the third time. Germany
wanted world power. Einstein gathered the living
dead and nothing would be normal ever again …

Jack Percival (10)
King's Road Primary School, Dunfermline

The Superdog

'Bye,' said Jane. She was going on holiday and left Buddy behind. Buddy, the dog, was actually a superdog and was taking care of the house. One night a robber sneaked in, but his tiptoes were no match for Buddy so he dashed and blew him away.

Marc Lovell (10)

King's Road Primary School, Dunfermline

The Cat

Thud! The cat fell off the table. He was asleep
but he must have rolled off the table. He was so
startled he jumped onto the lamp. He fell off and
took the lamp with him. *Smash!* When Mum gets
home he's in big trouble!

Melissa Emmerson (10)

King's Road Primary School, Dunfermline

142

Jack And The Beanstalk

Jack was going to see what was up the beanstalk, but a sudden shake and Jack fell into the beanstalk. As quick as a flash he fell in. Then the giant stood on the beanstalk and died.

Louis Douglas (10)
King's Road Primary School, Dunfermline

Burger Boy

One day Burger Boy turned back into a burger.
He went into his mum's room. She was alone.
He hid in the shadows, then he jumped out and
grabbed her. She woke up and hit him, then she
put him in the basement.

Kirsten Munro (11)
Kirkfieldbank Primary School, Kirkfieldbank

Walking Home Alone

Not long after the summer holidays, a girl called
Kelly came to town. Her home was in the middle
of the woods and she heard a noise so she went
out to see what it was. She came back in the
house and heard the noise again and again and …

Nicole Williamson (9)
Kirkfieldbank Primary School, Kirkfieldbank

145

Jack J Cameron And The House Elf Alfie

As he lay in his bed, Jack J Cameron sat up.
'What in the name of Afghanistan was that?' The
door to Jack's room smashed open. Sleepy Jack
caught sight of a fidgety little elf-like creature.
'Who are you?' hesitated Jack.
'I'm Alfie, the house elf!'

Victoria Wilson (9)
Kirkfieldbank Primary School, Kirkfieldbank

Untitled

One stormy night I got the fright of my life. I was walking through the house, it was dark and murky.

'Boo!'

'What the … what was that? Hello, who … who … who's there?'

'It's only me,' said a familiar voice.

'You're a monster!'

'No.'

'An alien?'

'No!'

'Oops, it's only Adam.'

Alastair Gourlay (11)
Kirkfieldbank Primary School, Kirkfieldbank

147

The Boy Who Dressed As An Alien

It was twelve o'clock at night, I was all alone at home. I went into my bedroom. I heard some noise. I went to my wardrobe.

'Boo!'

'Argh!' It was an alien. I ran down the stairs.

'Boo!'

'Argh!' It was Alastair then the alien came - but it was Wayne!

Oliver Sneddon (10)
Kirkfieldbank Primary School, Kirkfieldbank

Nellie The Dragon

I discovered a friendly little dragon called Nellie.
The village kids loved her and sat on her back and
fed her.
Then one day a gigantic dragon flew in. The
villagers were terrified of the new arrival.
Roar! The villagers fell back as a giggle came from
the dragon.

Kirsti McWhinnie (11)
Kirkfieldbank Primary School, Kirkfieldbank

The Computer Game

'Argh!' roared Jake with fright. He was down on the laminated flooring pleading for his life because he'd finished Level 3 on the Scary Maze game.
'What's wrong?' said Jake's mum.
'Nothing,' said Jake.
'You're playing that Scary Maze game again after I told you not to play it!'

Wayne Shillan (10)
Kirkfieldbank Primary School, Kirkfieldbank

Walking Home Alone

One freezing night at 12pm Sam was jogging
through the woods. He was nearly home. He was
getting scared. He thought there were hands. He
could see his home. He started to run but he fell.
Suddenly something touched his shoulder.
'Boo!' said Bob. 'I'll walk you home.'

Lewis Wilson (11)
Kirkfieldbank Primary School, Kirkfieldbank

My Teachers Are Aliens

As Kate passed through the creepy gate at the
front of Kirkfieldbank Primary School, she found
herself looking at a green slimy hand reaching for
her from the window. Kate tiptoed inside. She
looked in the staffroom and saw slimy aliens. She
blinked and ran down the hill.

Carrie Elliot (11)
Kirkfieldbank Primary School, Kirkfieldbank

The Adventures Of Pete Za Hut Part Two

It was eight o'clock and Pete Za Hut was playing his PlayStation. Suddenly there was a creaking noise. Frantically, he bolted upright.
'Boo!' It was his big brother Sean. 'I got you! he said. Even Pete burst out laughing because it was just a joke.

Adam Murray (10)
Kirkfieldbank Primary School, Kirkfieldbank

Lewis' Birthday Party

One morning at 11am Lewis was walking home
alone. What was that? He glanced at something.
Halfway down the road he saw it again. When he
got down the road he walked into his house.
'Surprise! Happy birthday.' He had a party and it
was great.

Lewis Naismith (10)
Kirkfieldbank Primary School, Kirkfieldbank

Katie's Surprise

Just managing to see her way along the path,
Katie approached the gravel path of her home.
Suddenly the lights of her house went *pop*. Katie
froze but somehow her legs carried her to the
door.
'Surprise!' It was Katie's birthday party with her
friends and family.

Jenna Stewart (9)
Kirkfieldbank Primary School, Kirkfieldbank

155

The Best Birthday Ever

Sleepily, I staggered into the kitchen to get my
breakfast. I plopped down to eat it and nearly fell
off my chair. Mum had leapt out with Dad and
roared, 'Happy birthday!' A beautiful Shetland
pony stuck its head in the window.
'Yes!' I screeched.

Lucy Tennant (9)
Kirkfieldbank Primary School, Kirkfieldbank

Harry Plopper And The Foreign Doughnut

Thump, thump, thump!
'Plopper! Get down here! Your mother and I are
going to the all you can eat buffet.'
'Snort,' Harry said as he put his glasses on.
Harry met with his friends.
'Have you heard of the foreign doughnut?' the
two wizard pigs said.
'Mmm, doughnuts,' Harry drooled.

Jamie Lee Wilson (10)
Kirkfieldbank Primary School, Kirkfieldbank

157

The Monster Who Was Afraid Of Children

One dark night the monster crawled under a bed
to settle for the night. *Creak!* A boy was going to
bed. Urg the monster quivered, he was afraid.
Doof! The boy leaped onto the bed.
'Ouch!' cried Urg.
'What was that?' the boy murmured.
'Me!'
The boy jumped and scurried off.

Liam Wilson (11)
Kirkfieldbank Primary School, Kirkfieldbank

158

The Boy Who Got Hit

Bravely, John swept to his aunt's house on a winter day. It was like being controlled because something made his hand open the door. 'Argh!' Something hit his face. John grabbed the thing! 'Is that? No, it can't be …a bat wearing a dress! I think my aunt's gone berserk!'

Kirsty McCreadie (10)
Kirkfieldbank Primary School, Kirkfieldbank

Caught Up

Phew, pant! 'I think we lost him.' Then they heard
the cracking of twigs, they froze to the spot with
fear. There was a legend about the monster of
these woods. The cracking got nearer and then
something leapt at Alex.
'Tig! Ha! Ha! You're it!'

Cameron Pollock (11)
Kirkfieldbank Primary School, Kirkfieldbank

The Awesome Scott

Vroom went the motorbike. Scott was riding round a very hard track. Round the corner he went, overtaking Alexander, and over the finish line he went.

The crowd was cheering, 'Go Scott' and 'You're the best!' Scott's family was very proud and the trophy was giant.

Chloe Ann Russell (9)
Lawmuir Primary School, Bellshill

The Evil Gummy Bear

Ding-dong! She opened the door. As her
eyes swirled, the evil gummy bear blasted
his strawberry flavourings and she became
hypnotised. Suddenly a huge gust of wind blew,
the door slammed shut and she ran to safety
upstairs. Suddenly she awoke - it was all a dream.

Julia Lappin (8)
Lawmuir Primary School, Bellshill

162

The Little Orphan

There once was an orphan who had no home and nothing to eat. She lived in a box under a bridge next to a river. Her name was Kara. She only had one thing to wear. Everyone ignored her when she was trying to get money for food and drink.

Nicole Findlay (8)
Lawmuir Primary School, Bellshill

The Wag-Tail Puppy

Maybe if I am really quick she'll see me! *Woof, woof*, please pick me!
'Look Daddy, at the dog with the black eye patch,' said Minnie.
She's looking at me, wag tail, wag! Put on puppy eyes.
'He's called Barney, Daddy, can I have him, please?'
'Why yes, you can!'

Nadia Dawson (10)
Lawmuir Primary School, Bellshill

Ice Cream City

Ice Cream City is full of cone-shaped people. The plants are made of mint ice cream and the houses are mint chocolate covered wafers. Even though it's full of ice cream it still manages to stay sunny. Confusing the king was named King Mint, he was called, 'Your Mintasty.'

Cerys Mitchell (10)
Lawmuir Primary School, Bellshill

Me And My Dog

Once I was in my bed sleeping and this man came into my bedroom and wiggled a wand at my head. The next morning my mum woke me up for school. I'd turned into a dog! I didn't know what to do.

Chloe Mckenzie (10)
Lawmuir Primary School, Bellshill

A Night In A Horrifying Bedroom

It was a dark, spooky, horrid night and Lindy-Lou
was in her bedroom. She heard a creaking noise
as the curtains blew by at the window. The lights
flickered, the tree made a shadow of a monster.
Lindy-Lou was so petrified she nearly jumped out
of her skin.

Rachel Allan (10)
Lawmuir Primary School, Bellshill

The Magic Seed

One day a boy named Sam was standing in his garden. He was planting seeds for his gran and he fell asleep.
The next day he went out and he saw a pumpkin. He said to himself, 'I planted a sunflower.'
He called friends over, they said, *'Wow!'*

Kayla Agnis Bolton (8)
Lawmuir Primary School, Bellshill

Pencil And Ruler

There was once a pencil with a friend, Ruler.
Pencil was going to Ruler's house; he got used
for maths, so he was tired. He eventually went to
Ruler's house and had a nice cup of rubber. The
black gel pen came in and threw him in the metric
sharpener.

Kim Jackson (8)
Lawmuir Primary School, Bellshill

YoungWriters

Batkor's Deadly House

He stood at the door and rang the bell. The door
suddenly moved and swept open. He stepped in
the house and the door closed, and behind him
was Batkor. Batkor grabbed the boy but as the
boy was picked up he heard something …
'Wake up, it's just a dream.'

David John Gault (9)
Lawmuir Primary School, Bellshill

170

Be Your Own Star

Lucy was a ten-year-old girl. She was looking up
at the stars and said, 'I want to be a star.'
A star replied, 'Be your own star.' So she tried to
fly and it worked.
She said, 'I'm flying!' And then she fell and woke
up.

Kirsten Muir (8)
Lawmuir Primary School, Bellshill

The Fish Who Couldn't Make Fire

Down in the deep blue sea, there was a fish called
Bob. He had just come back from work. He was
going to have a barbecue. He got all the best
firewood, but they kept dying.
His friends came round and said, 'You live in the
water.'
'Oh!'

Lauren Cameron Quinn (9)
Lawmuir Primary School, Bellshill

172

The Town Of Bellshill

The town of Bellshill sleeps as much as it can ever sleep, for Bellshill is a busy place day in, day out. The street is narrow and dirty, not bigger than an alleyway. The houses are nice with black roofs and the houses are made with plaster and red stones.

Billy Allan (9)
Lawmuir Primary School, Bellshill

My Birthday

I woke up in the morning before anyone else.
I hunted for my presents. I woke Mum at ten
to seven. I got BattleZone games and Jumping
Beans. My cake was made of chocolate, cream
and Smarties. I squished cream on my mum and
sister. My birthday was really great.

Ryan Mclean (10)
Lawmuir Primary School, Bellshill

The Night Out

One day I went to stay with Chloe Russell and we had so much fun. When it was time for bed, me and Chloe watched some DVDs and one was Home Alone 2 and it was so funny. We went to bed sidewards and woke up straight. So funny.

Rebecca Alex Linda Todd (9)
Lawmuir Primary School, Bellshill

175

The Birthday Girl

A little girl called Jennifer was looking out the
window and said to herself, 'It's my birthday!'
And then a big hairy monster came up and said,
'Happy birthday.' She got a fright. He said, 'I am a
friendly monster not a scary, scary monster,' and
she cuddled him.

Jennifer Norma Bridgeen Callaghan (9)
Lawmuir Primary School, Bellshill

The Vengeance Of Freddy Krueger

Freddy Krueger and Jason were fighting for power against each other. Jason knew Krueger's weak spot. Finally the battle began. Jason hit Krueger with his knife; Krueger tried a trick with his claws. Freddy Krueger hit Jason with one big blow. Jason collapsed. Freddy finished Jason off. Jason is now dead.

Jack John Wynn (8)
Lawmuir Primary School, Bellshill

Girl And Dog Go For Walk

Nine-year-old Emma takes her dog out for a walk. She sees something strange. She goes over to it. It's a slide burning. The dog goes into the fire; it doesn't harm the dog, so Emma goes in, too. It doesn't harm her. The fire doesn't harm anything.

Lucy Elizabeth Foye (8)
Lawmuir Primary School, Bellshill

The Vengeance Of Jason

Freddy Krueger and Jason were fighting each other for power. Jason knew Krueger's weak spot. Finally the battle began. Freddy Krueger bashed Jason with his claws. Jason used his knife to defend himself from the claws. Jason jumped high above Krueger and slit Krueger's neck. Jason won the battle.

Matthew James Foye (8)
Lawmuir Primary School, Bellshill

The Battle

One day Freddy Krueger was fighting with
Michael Myers. Someone passing by phoned the
police. The police burst through the door. Michael
said, 'We're going to go together.'
Freddy said, 'OK.' So they slashed the police. The
police didn't stop coming - Freddy Krueger and
Michael Myers were arrested.

Aidan McRobert (8)
Lawmuir Primary School, Bellshill

Halloween

I woke up, my room was dark. I looked around
me. I could see the Halloween decorations sitting
in my room. I shouted to Mum, 'It's Halloween,
can we go trick or treating?'
'Yes, we can, let's go then.' It was fun. I went out
as a vampire.

Emma Robertson (9)
Lawmuir Primary School, Bellshill

The Mystery Beast

It was a scary night when Mary saw the beast.
It was eight metres tall. It had red, angry eyes,
brown fur and black claws.
The next day Mary went to the library to look at
the book of beasts. She found out the beast was a
rare polyphemus Cyclops.

Ethan Kar kin Cheung (9)
Lawmuir Primary School, Bellshill

The Blood Of The Hound

It started in the wood. I was walking and I heard rattling. It was behind the bush. I saw its shadow. It jumped out. It was my friend, he said, 'Got ya!' Then a bloodhound dripping with blood, twice the usual size, barked and chased us like mad.

Darryl Holland (9)
Lawmuir Primary School, Bellshill

Winning Rugby

One day I went to rugby and we won. So we got
a medal and trophy for the team.
When I got home I could not see anyone, so I
told my dad and then everyone jumped out and
said congratulations for winning and I was so, so
happy.

Tony Cunningham (9)

Lawmuir Primary School, Bellshill

Annoying Sister

There was a boy called Stephen, he had a sister,
she was annoying. There was a tap on the door.
There was no one there.
'There it goes again,' said Stephen. He didn't
answer it. It went again. He looked, he saw her -
it was his sister. He said, *'Rrr!'*

Bayley McGuire Brown (9)
Lawmuir Primary School, Bellshill

A Not So Scary Tale

It was time for a jog on Friday 13th, the girl
picked up some speed through a tunnel. Starting
to go faster, she fell and saw a man in black, but it
was just a jogger. She was okay so she ran back to
her house safe and sound.

Amy Walsh (9)
Lawmuir Primary School, Bellshill

My Life

I was in my room playing the computer when suddenly I heard my mum shouting for dinner. We were having pie.
Once I was finished, I went to play the computer. I was playing Call of Duty when I heard a bang on the door - I was scared ...

Kai Rooney (9)
Lawmuir Primary School, Bellshill

The Woods

I went to the woods and I saw a stone next to a
leprechaun. He gave me a pot of gold.
I said, 'No.' Then I saw a diamond. 'That's nice,' I
went to get it. It puffed into a cloud of smoke and
was never seen again.

Marc Shilliday (9)
Lawmuir Primary School, Bellshill

When Charlie Was Born

The day my little cousin Charlie was born was the most exciting day of my life. He was the cutest baby in the world, and has brought lots of fun and laughter into our family. I really hope he will grow up to be just like me and my brothers.

Oliver Hickson (9)
Lawmuir Primary School, Bellshill

The Cold-Handed Man

There once was a man who had cold hands. He
lived in a cold town but he didn't have any gloves.
One day it had been one of the coldest days in
years. His mum bought him a pair of gloves for his
birthday, his hands were never cold again.

Colin Cupples (11)
Lawmuir Primary School, Bellshill

Scared

My knees are trembling, my heart is pounding.
There are goosebumps running down my back.
Nowhere to run, nowhere to hide. It is truly
frightening to my eyes. I curl up into a ball, close
my eyes to hide what's there. This is what I do
when I am scared.

Tom Gallagher (11)
Lawmuir Primary School, Bellshill

191

Predator

In the depths of North America, in the mountains,
there lives a bear with a fearsome attitude.
He lumbers out of his cave and makes his way
towards the river. He stands in there waiting for
the salmon to jump. *Snap!* The jaws of the bear
close over the salmon.

Lewis Goddard (10)
Lawmuir Primary School, Bellshill

The Shark's Den!

A school of fish were passing by, when *aah!* They
noticed a big hungry-looking shark.
'No, wait, I'm not going to eat you but would you
like to come to my den?'
'OK,'
His den was amazing, it had toys and games, but
best of all candy. 'Want some?'

Morgan Mitchell (10)
Lawmuir Primary School, Bellshill

Happy Halloween

It was the 31st of October. Tom and Katie were
out trick or treating. They went to a big scary
house at the end of Cherry Tree Street. They
knocked on the big black door. A tall skinny man
came to the door …
Katie and Tom ran back home.

Toni-Elana Clemenson (10)

Lawmuir Primary School, Bellshill

Mr Rubber Gets Lost In The Woods

One day Mr Rubber went down the forest
when he heard a noise. He said, 'I'm scared of
darkness.' He walked along then he heard it again,
then he said to himself, 'I want to go home.' So he
walked along then he was home.

Chloe Hogg (9)
Lawmuir Primary School, Bellshill

The Evil Dog

There once lived a Doberman that bit everyone
that he saw. He had bloodshot eyes and razor-
sharp white teeth that were packed inside his
strong jaw. He once bit someone very hard and
killed them. From then on no one dared to even
go by the dangerous street.

Yasmin Daniels (10)
Lawmuir Primary School, Bellshill

Untitled

My family and I were watching TV. I was scared. It was dark. I saw lots of shadows around me. It was scary. I turned around, my parents were not there! I realised they were in bed.

Adam Henry (8)
Park Primary School, Stranraer

One Night Out

One night I went to Loch Ness for a picnic. I
took out my baguette and I went to eat it, it
disappeared. I looked behind me in fear. I heard
something in front of me! It was a cat. It stole my
lunch. *Phew!*

Morgan White (8)
Park Primary School, Stranraer

198

The Scariest Holiday Of My Life

As I went down I saw this mysterious shadow.
It was black with black scars on its face. I was
petrified. I tried to swim as fast as I could but I
just realised it was my papa in a disguise.

Robert Dargie (8)
Park Primary School, Stranraer

The Man In Hospital

I saw a man on the hospital floor, he was rolling
about crazily! I thought he was having a fit and
going to die. He screamed. I ran over to help.
The man shouted, 'I've just won the lottery!'
Phew!

Katie Mae Hardie (9)
Park Primary School, Stranraer

Scared

I was in my bed, I saw mysterious shadows
outside. I was scared.
'Argh! Help!' I shouted to my dad.
He didn't believe me! He said, 'Go back to sleep.'
Just then I realised it was my brother playing
tricks on me.

Tracianne Smith (8)
Park Primary School, Stranraer

Dinosaur Madness

Once I was exploring the beach when I saw movement under the sand. *What is that?* I thought. I moved close and something jumped out at me. 'Argh!' I screamed. 'It's a parasurolophus and a T-rex!'
Out of the hole came their babies and I never returned.

Heather McCreadie
Park Primary School, Stranraer

My Father!

When I went to bed I heard shrieking. I was petrified. I was shaking. I was frozen to the ground. I got out of bed and checked all the rooms and cupboards and drawers. I went into my dad's room and it was only my dad snoring.

Dylan Palmer
Park Primary School, Stranraer

The Dragons

Dragons swooped through the sky, blowing fire at everyone. They knocked down buildings and smashed cars. They made a wreck of the city before leaving the city alone. As they flew away, one puffed out one more giant ball of fire, this ball of fire killed everyone except one person.

Andrea Patterson (10)

Reston Primary School, Eyemouth

204

The Rescue

Kara lay on the freezing cold floor of the dungeon
hoping that she would get the chance to survive
when a noise came approaching her. It sounded
like … footsteps coming closer. Kara whispered a
prayer to herself.
Then came the voice, 'I'm here to rescue you.'

Lara Fitzpatrick Ward (10)
Reston Primary School, Eyemouth

205

In Rome

This story begins in 1842 in Rome with two girls called Floriana and Cassia. Floriana was 14 and Cassia was almost 9. They were sisters and they both had a best friend called Paulina and she was 16 coming up for 17 years old and they played together with dolls.

Cara Dixon (8)

St Anthony's Primary School, Rutherglen

206

Scared

Creak! What was that? 'Is someone there?' The lights flickered on and off. I walked into the kitchen. *I didn't open the fridge,* I thought to myself. The door creaked open. *Woof.*
'Oh, it was you Scruffy.'
Bang! Clash!
'What was that?' A deafening noise came from the old attic.

Catherine McCready (10)
St Anthony's Primary School, Rutherglen

The Stranger

Knock, knock, knock. I got out of bed. I walked slowly downstairs. *Knock, knock, knock, knock.* I opened the door, nobody was there. I ran to the kitchen, picked up the frying pan and went into the hall. *Bang* …oh dear, it was only my dad.

Ian Dickson (10)
St Anthony's Primary School, Rutherglen

The Fake Alien Invasion

They are coming, the invasion has started. The aliens will conquer the Earth. I am going to die. They are destroying the city. The aliens are across the road. Wait a minute; they are leaving with a sandwich. They must have been hungry. Poor, poor aliens. I'll miss them.

Steven Glancy (10)
St Anthony's Primary School, Rutherglen

My Friend Hates Me

My friend hates me now. Why? I didn't mean to hit her! Maybe I could ask her? Well, it didn't go well. Maybe our friendship is really over! Good riddance! Why should we be friends? I'll make a new friend. I don't need her.
Okay, I really need her. Happy!

Grace Fallon (10)
St Anthony's Primary School, Rutherglen

Pranked

'Ha, ha,' said a young Scots boy. 'I pranked you,' he laughed.
While he walked home he passed a loch, its waters were still and calm. Then something juddered the water. He was uneasy. 'Monster!' 'Ya, ye have been pranked,' said a man. ''Twas only a fallin' rock, ha, ha!'

Kane Caldwell (10)
St Anthony's Primary School, Rutherglen

Untitled

Drip, drip, drip. 'What was that?' I whispered to myself. I looked behind me, nothing was there. Mum and Dad were out, I couldn't run to them. *Drip, drip, drip.* There was that noise again. I stood completely still. I looked down to the floor … it was a tiny mouse!

Chantelle Collins (10)
St Anthony's Primary School, Rutherglen

Happy Family

Three sisters lived in a care home, their names:
Tee, Louise and Tracy. They had a little sister,
Poppy. Tee and Louise were 10 years old, Tracy
was 5 and Poppy was 3. They were upset about
living in a care home. Then they all got fostered.
They were all very happy.

Emma Donnelly (10)
St Anthony's Primary School, Rutherglen

Homer's Dream Come True

Homer heard the rain battering against his
bedroom window.
'Oh Marge, it's not rain, it's beer,' he cried,
crashing downstairs in his underpants. Rushing
outside, Homer flung back his head and opened
his mouth to gulp down the golden dream.
'Wake up Homer - I've left the shower on for
you.'

Shannon Sweeney (9)
St Anthony's Primary School, Rutherglen

The Scary School

It was a cold and stormy morning and the boys and girls were scared. Connor, Taylor and Jude were frightened as well. They heard a bang and the teacher came in and said, 'You need to go home.' The storm got even worse and they all went home.

Ryan McKay (8)
St Anthony's Primary School, Rutherglen

Dinosaur Wrestling

Ding! Ding! Round one. *Bang! Boom!* 'Dino! Dino! Dino!' *Booom!* Game over! Dino won! The crowd went wild.
Dino went home. His dad was watching him on the TV. 'Well done Son,' said Dino's dad. 'Ya wanna wrestle?' he said. 'What's wrong, ya chicken? *Bawk, bawk.*' He turned and fought.

Michael Lochran (8)
St Anthony's Primary School, Rutherglen

216

The Burning Of Rome

One day Mark said, 'I want to go to Rome.'
We couldn't go, but we could go to Milan. So we
did go to Milan. When we got there, we went
to Milan then the city of Rome. Then Mark died.
Then the city of Rome got destroyed.

Kieran Evans (8)
St Anthony's Primary School, Rutherglen

Pooh Bear And The Magic Honey

One day Pooh saw some sparkly honey that made
him gaze at it. It suddenly took him to Honey
World! He ate and ate and ate and was so chubby
but it turned out it was all a dream. He also told
all his friends and they believed his story.

Jason Kirk (8)
St Anthony's Primary School, Rutherglen

The Olympics

One day my dad went to the Olympics and he said, 'I can run faster than that!' So he ran to Olympic Park and started to run fast. Then he got up to the top and then he started to fall and a person called Jim helped him.

Megan Devine (8)
St Anthony's Primary School, Rutherglen

The Chocolate World

Once there was a chocolate world. It was raining
in the north and the south but this was the
west. It was very sunny in the west but just then
appeared a rainbow, it was beautiful. They all sang
a song about a rainbow and they lived happily
ever after.

Shannon Jackson (8)
St Anthony's Primary School, Rutherglen

God Came To Tea

One day Beth and her mum Cara were having tea. One minute later there was a knock at the door. Beth went to the door, at the door there was a strange man. Beth asked her mum, 'Who is that strange man?'
'I do not know Beth.'

Kayleigh Islip (8)
St Anthony's Primary School, Rutherglen

Dumbo

Once upon a time in a magical land a baby
elephant was born. His name was Dumbo and he
was a very special baby. He had a yellow hat on
his head.
Two years later Dumbo had big ears. He started
to flap his ears. He was flying! He's unbelievable!

Mark Kirk (8)
St Anthony's Primary School, Rutherglen

The White Wall

A man called Alfred, he lived for several years,
then he had a boy called Tristian. He always
wanted to cross the wall.
One day he crossed the wall, he did not come
back for 10 years.
1 month later he came back, the man died 10
years later, *ohh*.

Beth McAlister (8)
St Anthony's Primary School, Rutherglen

223

Pat The Artist

In France there was a man called Pat and he was
very good at art. In fact he was excellent at art.
He met Van Gogh and Jack Vettriano.
One day he went out for a walk and do you know
who he met? Da Vinci, painting the Mona Lisa.

Jude Thornton (8)
St Anthony's Primary School, Rutherglen

A Day In The Life Of Club Penguin

Once there was a world of penguins but these were not any old penguins, these were club penguins. It was one of the penguin birthdays, the penguin's name was Fire Red 102. When he came to his igloo his friends were there.
'Happy birthday,' they shouted.
Fire Red was stunned.

Ciaran McMorrow (9)
St Teresa's Primary School, Newarthill

225

The Mad Scientist

Once upon a time there was a mad scientist who wanted to destroy the world so he built a bomb. He was nearly finished when he was captured by aliens. Some say he caused the Roswell Incident trying to escape. Is this true? No one will ever know.

Murray Telfer (11)
St Teresa's Primary School, Newarthill

226

A Scary Tale

Once in the land of strange there was a young boy who wandered the woods. It was getting dark. Suddenly he heard a loud voice. He saw a blue ghost. He ran and ran back to the town but, sadly, if you go into the woods, you don't come back.

Marcus McGinn (9)
St Teresa's Primary School, Newarthill

Simpson - Homer Simpson

Last year in Springfield, Homer was sitting on the couch. Next thing, someone knocked the door. It was James Bond. 'Is this Ned Flanders?' said James.
'No, he lives next door,' Homer replied.
'Thanks,' said James. 'He has hacked into the government and tried to find out all our secrets.'

Sean Bradley (10)
St Teresa's Primary School, Newarthill

Clumsy Rooney

There was a little bunny called Clumsy Rooney
and he always did silly things. It was the Easter
holidays and he had to deliver Easter eggs. He
was missing a few. He searched everywhere; he
didn't find any so he popped to the shop and just
bought the rest.

Nathan Speirs (10)
St Teresa's Primary School, Newarthill

Day Brightener

In fifteen minutes I will launch a giant flower at Earth and no one can stop me, thought the man. Suddenly an MI5 agent came in and arrested him. He was taken to a special prison and served fourteen years with a new name of Van Der Sar.

Douglas Telfer

St Teresa's Primary School, Newarthill

230

Birthday Surprise

It was June. It was Kayleigh's special day, she was turning ten. She was very excited. Her parents went out. She was sleeping and woke up when they weren't there. There was a *bang!* She went to see what it was.
'Happy birthday!'
'That was great everyone, thanks very much.'

Kayleigh Hart (10)
St Teresa's Primary School, Newarthill

The Easter Bunny's Holiday

The Easter bunny was thinking to himself, *I deserve a holiday.* He packed a bag for his holidays. He thought about where he could go. He decided on Blackpool. He hopped all the way to Blackpool. When he arrived he was so shattered that he slept for the whole holiday.

Sam McCool (10)

St Teresa's Primary School, Newarthill

Beyond All Things Normal

I woke up in the forest by the lake. It was a dark night with the moon as my only light. It shone like a million stars. I didn't know how I got here but the darkness would never end. I saw something, was it me or the shadow girl?

Emma Cunningham (10)
St Teresa's Primary School, Newarthill

233

Little Lost Sally

A little girl called Sally was strolling through the forest, it was dark and quiet. She realised she would have to go home, but she couldn't find her way back so she found a nice cosy spot against the tree. She sat up looking at the stars and dozed off.

Robyn Clifford (10)
St Teresa's Primary School, Newarthill

Football Disaster

One day there was a great football player called Messi. He was the greatest footballer in the world. Everyone cheered when he scored. He played for Barcelona and Argentina.
Once he was playing Manchester United and Wayne Rooney broke his leg and after the game he was never seen again.

Paddy Conway (10)
St Teresa's Primary School, Newarthill

235

Humpty-Dumpty

Once upon a time there was an egg called
Humpty-Dumpty. He was happily playing in the
wood but then the mean Easter Bunny came
along. He chased him about the wood. When he
crashed into a tree he smashed into pieces.
'Yum,' said the bunny and ate him up.

Chloe Cunningham (10)
St Teresa's Primary School, Newarthill

A Day In The Life Of Abbi

My name is Abbi Mimnaugh and my favourite
thing is the Newarthill Gala Days. At every gala
day I go on the rides and enjoy every one of
them. They're such fun.
When it gets late and it's becoming dark, I head
home always thinking of the fun I've had.

Abbi Mimnaugh (10)
St Teresa's Primary School, Newarthill

237

That Dark Night

The whirling winds of that cold September evening sent chills down his spine. That night in the haunted house down in the middle of the dark forest there was a voice singing, it was getting closer and closer each time he turned round. He was never found ever again.

Naomi Presavage (10)
St Teresa's Primary School, Newarthill

Tiny Treasures Fiction From Southern Scotland

Information

We hope you have enjoyed reading this book - and that you will continue to enjoy it in the coming years.

If you like reading and writing, drop us a line or give us a call and we'll send you a free information pack. Alternatively visit our website at www.youngwriters.co.uk

Write to:
Young Writers Information,
Remus House,
Coltsfoot Drive,
Peterborough,
PE2 9JX

Tel: (01733) 890066
Email: youngwriters@forwardpress.co.uk